NUTS in SPACE

BADGER: SECURITY

DUCK MD: MEDICAL

OWL: CHIEF NAVIGATOR

FOX: POULTRY OFFICER

SQUIRREL: NUT EXPERT

BEAVER: ENGINEER

COMMANDER MOOSE

OPERATION: GATHER NUTS

NUT STORE

ATMOSPHERE TREES

BRIDGE

SLEEPING QUARTERS

LIBRARY AND LOUNGE

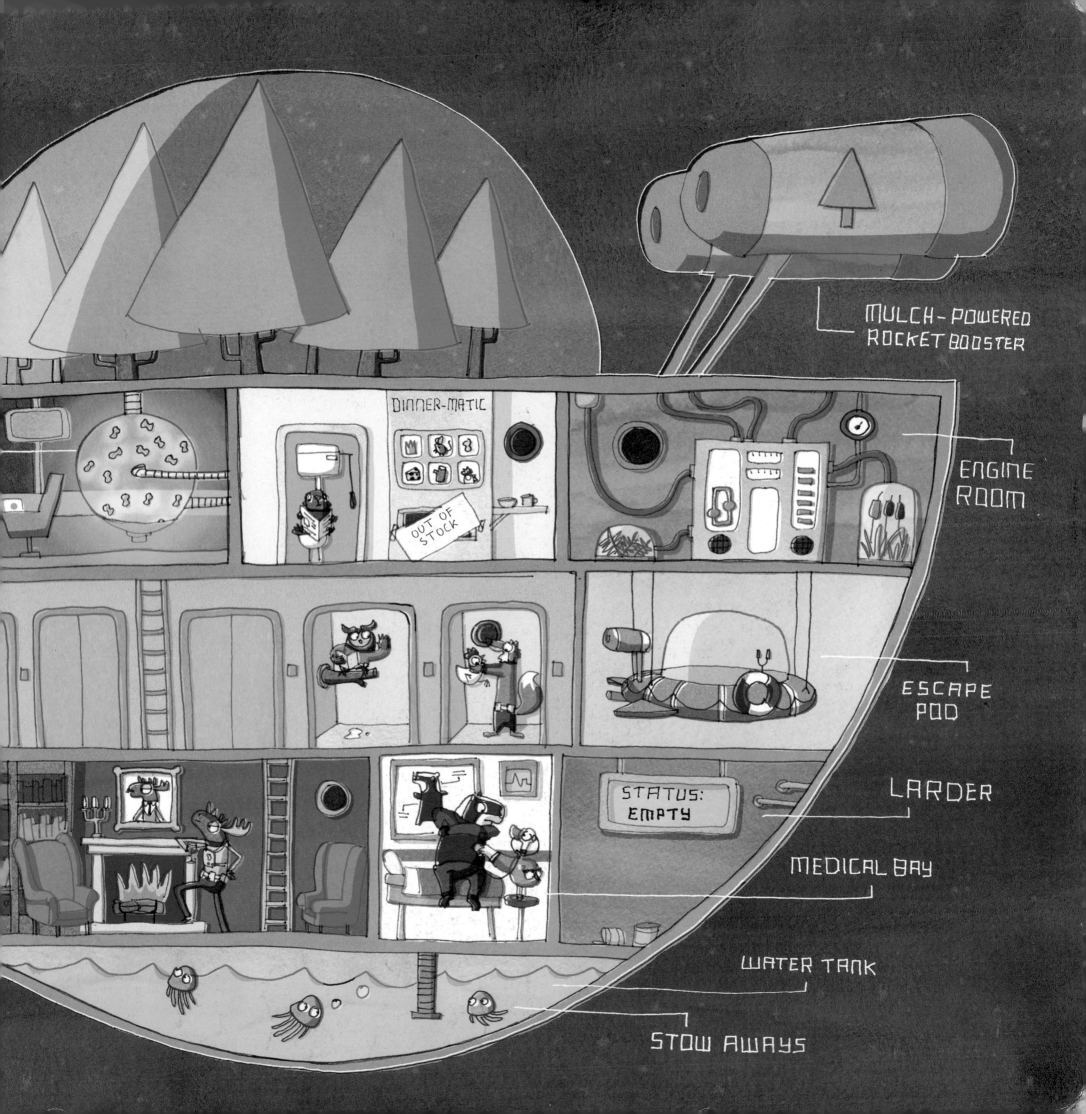

MULCH-POWERED ROCKET BOOSTER

DINNER-MATIC

OUT OF STOCK

ENGINE ROOM

ESCAPE POD

LARDER

STATUS: EMPTY

MEDICAL BAY

WATER TANK

STOW AWAYS

For Nora, Toby and my
hoard of siblings better known
as Joe, Paul, Tonia and Tim.

SUPER STEALTH COVERT CRUISER

FOREST FLEET 704

First published in 2014 by Nosy Crow Ltd. The Crow's Nest, 10a Lant Street, London SE1 1QR

www.nosycrow.com

This edition First published 2015

ISBN 978 0 85763 391 0

Nosy Crow and associated logos are trademarks and /or registered trademarks of Nosy Crow Ltd.

Text and illustration © Elys Dolan 2014

The right of Elys Dolan to be identified as the author and illustrator of this work has been asserted.

A CIP catalogue record for this book is available from the British Library.

Printed in China

1 3 5 7 9 8 6 4 2

It is written that at the very edge of deep space,
there can be found The Lost Nuts of Legend.
The bearer of this mythical snack will be immortal,
invincible and never will it be past their bedtime. BUT . . .

The Lost Nuts of Legend must never, EVER be eaten.

The crew of the Forest Fleet's finest Starship, a team

carefully chosen to find the nuts for the good of all

creaturekind, are now returning from their mission

triumphant, with the Nuts on board. The journey has been

long and hard, and now there is no food left. Everyone's

hungry and a bit grumpy. Luckily, all they have to do now is . . .

. . . GO HOME!

Oh look, floating words.

That's different.

Now that their mission is complete, and The Lost Nuts of Legend are on board, the crew has gathered in the Control Room to set a course for home.

But something has gone horribly wrong
with the Star Nav . . .

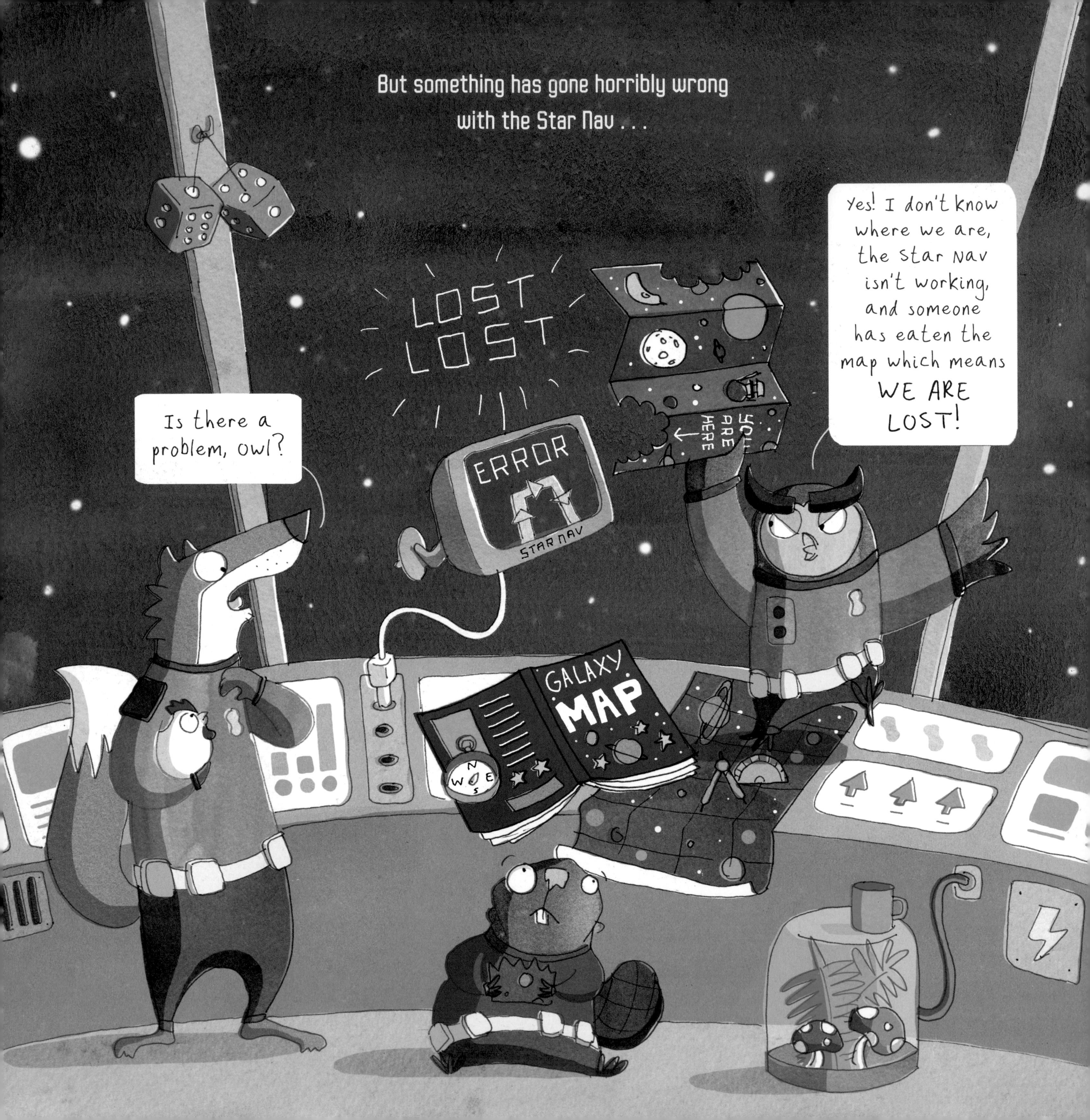

The crew ask for directions at the cafe but none of the regulars know The Way Home . . .
What do you mean, they're not serving food?!
Thank you! We're here all week.
It's nice to get out of the office.
JIM
Commander's log: space date - 128 days until Christmas. We have become lost on our return journey but have disembarked from the ship to ask for directions . . .
Freeze, alien!
What kind of crazy alien technology is this?
MENU Eat at Jim's
I'll always take care of you.

The Starship soon arrives at the small moon but it turns out the locals aren't too keen on Nuts.

The crew do as the Little Green Men suggest and go to ask at the forest planet down the road. The residents seem just delightful . . .

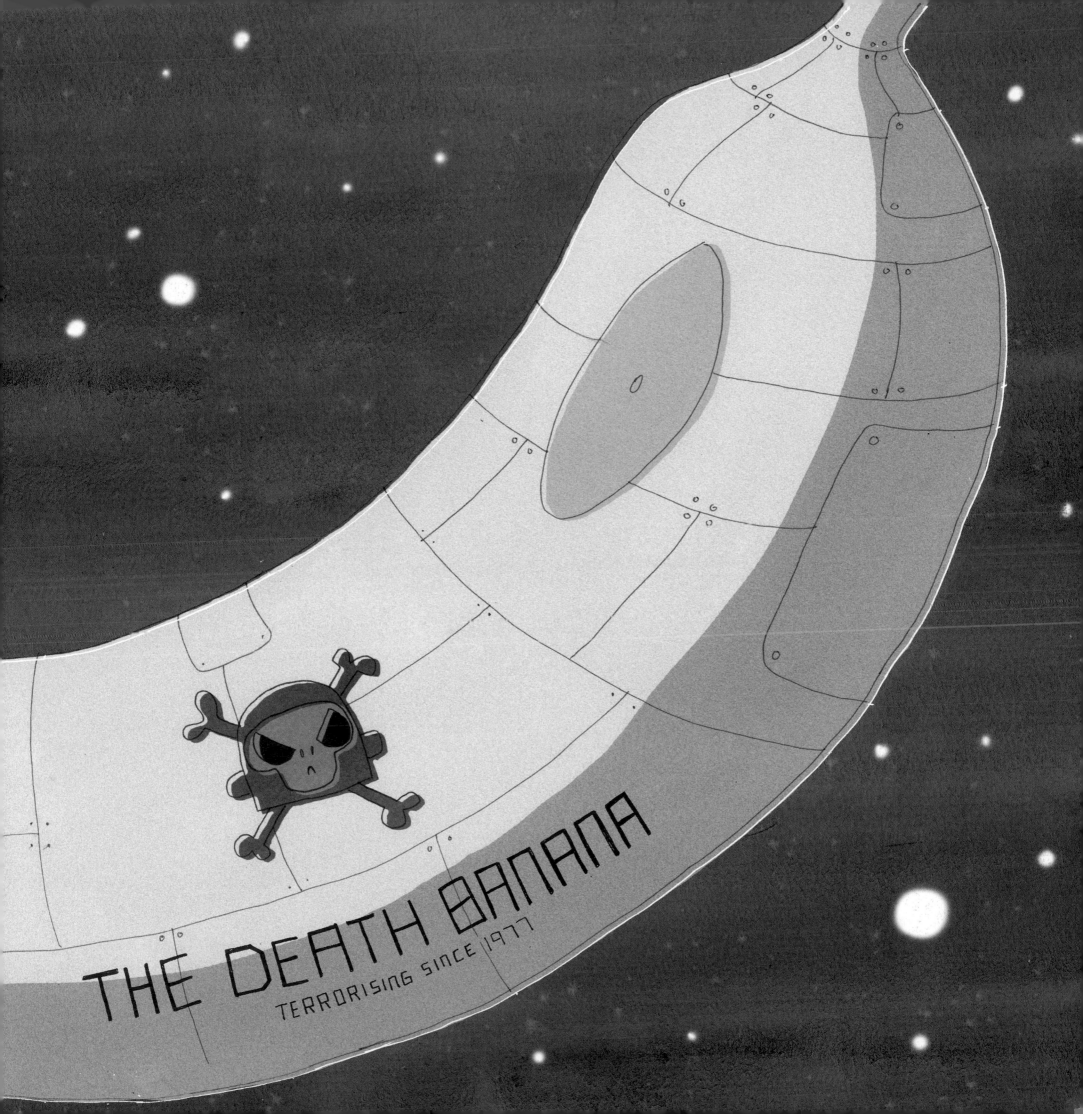

However, it turns out the monkeys are VERY interested in The Lost Nuts of Legend, so the crew make a hasty exit . . .

After their heroic escape from the Death Banana, everyone is very excited to be going Home . . .
HOME this way
Let's celebrate with a nice cup of tea!
MURRRPHMUR!
I can't wait to get Home! I'm going to write my autobiography and go on chat shows! What have you and your friend got planned, Fox?
BOSS
PANIC STATION

And so, with The Lost Nuts of Legend gone, our crew is left with only one choice – to turn the ship around and set off once again in search of more . . .
RIGHT! Turn around! It's time to boldly go where no animal has gone before, and get some more NUTS! AGAIN!
SUPER STEALTH COVERT CRUISER
FOREST FLEET 704
Err, I think Squirrel might need a moment.

. . . NUTS IN SPACE.

BADGER: SECURITY

DUCK MD: MEDICAL

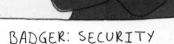

OWL: CHIEF NAVIGATOR

FOX: POULTRY OFFICER

SQUIRREL: NUT EXPERT

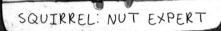

BEAVER: ENGINEER

COMMANDER MOOSE

OPERATION: GATHER NUTS

NUT STORE

ATMOSPHERE TREES

BRIDGE

SLEEPING QUARTERS

LIBRARY AND LOUNGE

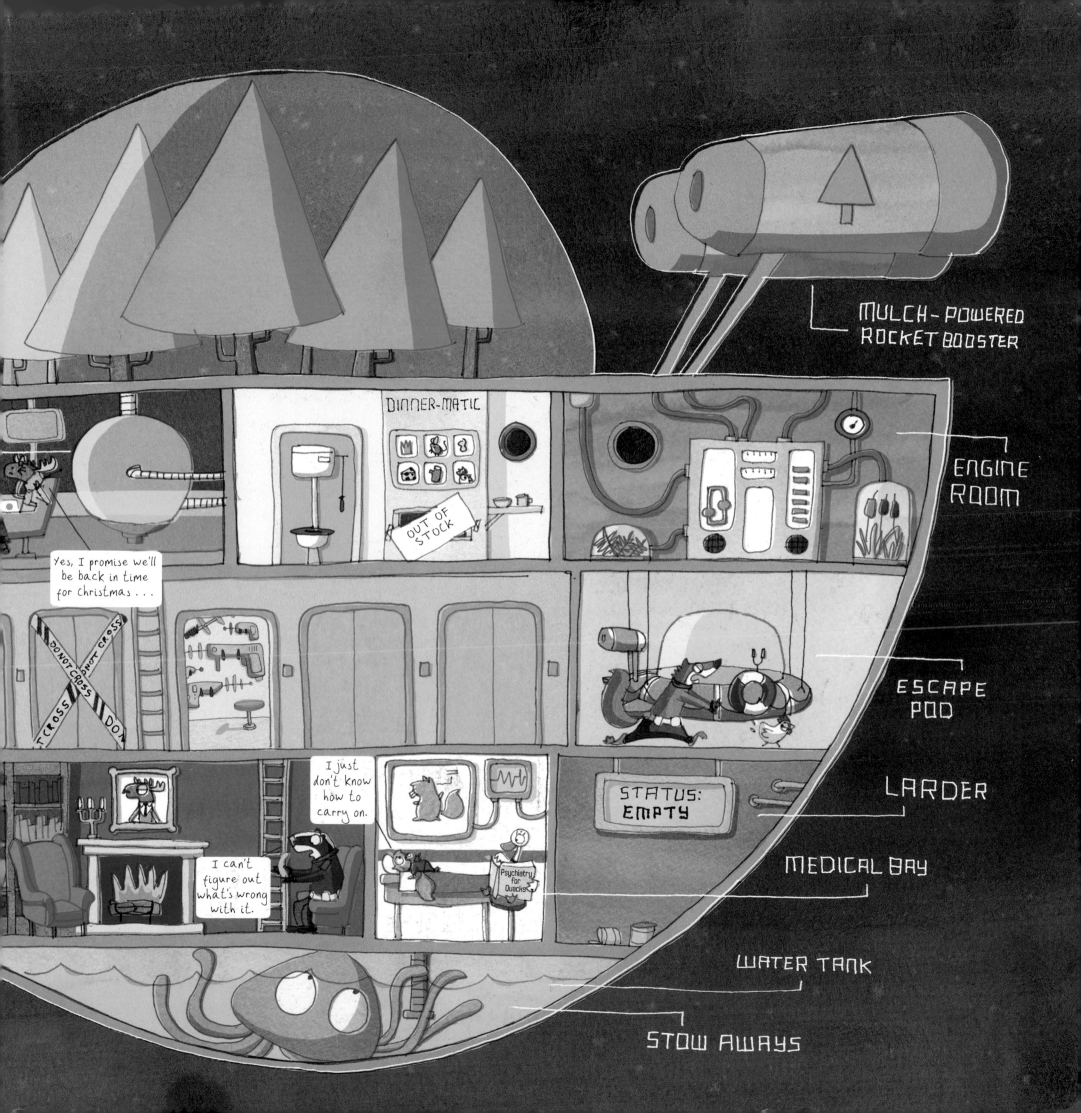